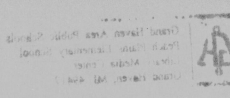

THE GOLDEN FLOWER

A TAINO MYTH FROM PUERTO RICO

by NINA JAFFE illustrated by ENRIQUE O. SÁNCHEZ

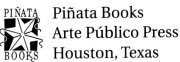

PIÑATA BOOKS

Piñata Books
Arte Público Press
Houston, Texas

Publication of *The Golden Flower: A Taino Myth from Puerto Rico* is made possible through support from the City of Houston through the Houston Arts Alliance. We are grateful for their support.

Piñata Books are full of surprises!

Piñata Books
An Imprint of Arte Público Press
University of Houston
452 Cullen Performance Hall
Houston, Texas 77204-2004

Jaffe, Nina
   The Golden Flower: A Taino Myth from Puerto Rico / retold by Nina Jaffe; illustrations by Enrique O. Sánchez.
        p.   cm.
   Summary: This myth explains the origin of the sea, the forest, and the island now called Puerto Rico.
   ISBN 978-1-55885-452-9 (alk. paper)
   [1. Taino Indians—Legends. 2. Tales—Puerto Rico. [Taino Indians—Legends.
2. Indians of the West Indies—Puerto Rico—Legends. 3. Creation—Folklore.
4. Folklore—Puerto Rico.] I. Sánchez, Enrique O., ill.   II. Title.
   F1969.J33   1996
   398.2'097295—dc20
   [E]   92-42364
                                                                                        CIP

∞ The paper used in this publication meets the requirements of the American National Standard for Permanence of Paper for Printed Library Materials, Z39.48-1984.

9 0 1 2 3 4 5 6 7 8   0 9 8 7 6 5 4 3 2

For Dania Vázquez—dear friend, gifted teacher—amiga de mi corazón.
—N. J.

For my editor, Soyung Pak
—E. O. S.

The author gratefully acknowledges Otilio Diaz, director of La Casa de La Herencia
Puertorriqueña in New York City, who reviewed the text for historical and linguistic accuracy
and detail. Special thanks are also due to Mari Haas at Teacher's College,
Columbia University, for her support and encouragement.

AFTERWORD

I first encountered this magical tale of the Taíno people in a Spanish text by Carmen Puigdollers.* I began to retell it in schools and libraries. In 1993, Lilian Ayala, a Spanish teacher in New York City, told me that she remembered hearing her mother tell this same story at family gatherings, when she was growing up in Puerto Rico. In my research, I learned that stories in which the sea was hidden inside a pumpkin (*calabaza*) were common among many of the native cultures in South America and the Caribbean.

The Taíno called their island home Boriquén (bo-ree-KEN), which means "land of the brave lord." They were a peaceful people who survived by hunting and fishing in the rich tropical forests and planting in their own fields. Their houses, called *bohíos* (bo-EE-ohs), were made of wood and cane roofed with straw. The Taíno chief was called a *cacique* (kah-SEE-kay), and it was he who told the myths and legends during the *areito* (ah-RAY-toh) ceremonies.

After Columbus landed his ships on the island's shore in 1493, the Spaniards conquered Boriquén. The Taíno were enslaved, and most of them died. Despite the destruction of their people, many words in Puerto Rico today come from the Taíno language. Taíno foods are still cooked, Taíno instruments are still played, and Puerto Ricans still proudly call their island "Borinquen" in honor of the Taíno heritage that is such an important part of their history and culture.

---

*Puigdollers, Carmen. "Como se formó la bella isla de Borinquen" in *Presencia Taína*. Cambridge, MA, National Assessment and Dissemination Center, Lesley College, 1979.

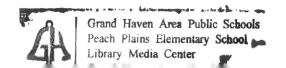

Long ago, the island of Puerto Rico was called *Boriquén.* This was the name given to it by the first people who lived there, the Taino. From time to time, the families in a Taino village would stop their work and gather together for a celebration called an *areito.* All through the night, they would dance and sing. Then young and old would gather together in a great circle and listen to stories of magic and wonder, of Taino heroes, and of how things came to be.

As you read this book, imagine that you, too, are sitting in this magic circle on a warm tropical night. The wind is blowing through the palm trees, the stars twinkle in the sky, and the storyteller begins to weave an ancient myth, a Taino tale from long ago. . . .

In the beginning of the world, there was no water anywhere
on earth. There was only a tall mountain that stood alone on
a wide desert plain.

There were no green plants. There were no flowers. All the
people lived on top of this mountain.

One day, a child went walking on the dry land below the mountain. As he bent down over the ground looking for food, something floated by on the wind. He reached out and caught it in his hand. It was a seed. A small, brown seed. He put the seed into his pouch.

The next day, he went walking, and again found something as it floated by on the wind. It was another seed. Day by day, he gathered these seeds until his pouch was full. It could not hold anymore. And the child said to himself, "I will plant these seeds at the top of our mountain."

He planted the seeds and waited. One morning, a tiny green leaf appeared. The child watched. From under the ground, a forest began to grow high on top of the mountain.

All the people came to see. It was a forest of many-colored flowers, a magic garden of green leaves and thick branches. The child was happy.

In the middle of the forest, at the foot of the tallest tree, there grew a vine that wrapped itself around the tree.

And from that vine there grew a flower more beautiful than all the rest. A bright flower with golden petals.

And from that flower, something new appeared in the forest.
It looked like a little ball. "Look!" cried the child. "Something is
growing out of the flower!"

As the people gathered around to watch, the ball grew larger and larger, until it became a great yellow globe that shone like the sun. Even as they walked on the dry land far below, people could see it shining on top of the mountain.

One woman said, "If you put your ear next to the ball, you can hear strange noises coming from inside." The people listened. Strange sounds and murmuring could be heard. But nobody knew what was hidden inside.

The people were afraid. After that, they all stayed away. Even the child stayed away.

One day, a man walking on the desert plain saw the golden ball. He said, "If that shining ball were mine, I would have the power of the sun. I could light up the sky, or make darkness fall." And he ran toward it, climbing up the rocky mountainside.

On the other side of the mountain, another man saw the shining globe, and he also said, "I want that thing for myself. It will give me great powers." He, too, began to run. Each one climbed quickly. Each one found a footpath that led to the tree.

They both ran without stopping until they reached the shining globe at the same time. But what they found was not really a ball; it was the fruit of the golden flower: a *calabaza*— a pumpkin.

The two men began to fight and argue.

"It is mine!" said one.

"No, it is mine!" said the other.

Each man grabbed the pumpkin. They pushed and pulled. They pulled and tugged until . . .

. . . finally, the vine broke. The pumpkin began to roll down the mountain faster and faster, until it crashed into a sharp rock and burst apart.

Whoosh! Waves of water poured out of the pumpkin. The water bubbled and foamed. The waves began to cover the earth, flooding the desert plain, rising higher and higher.

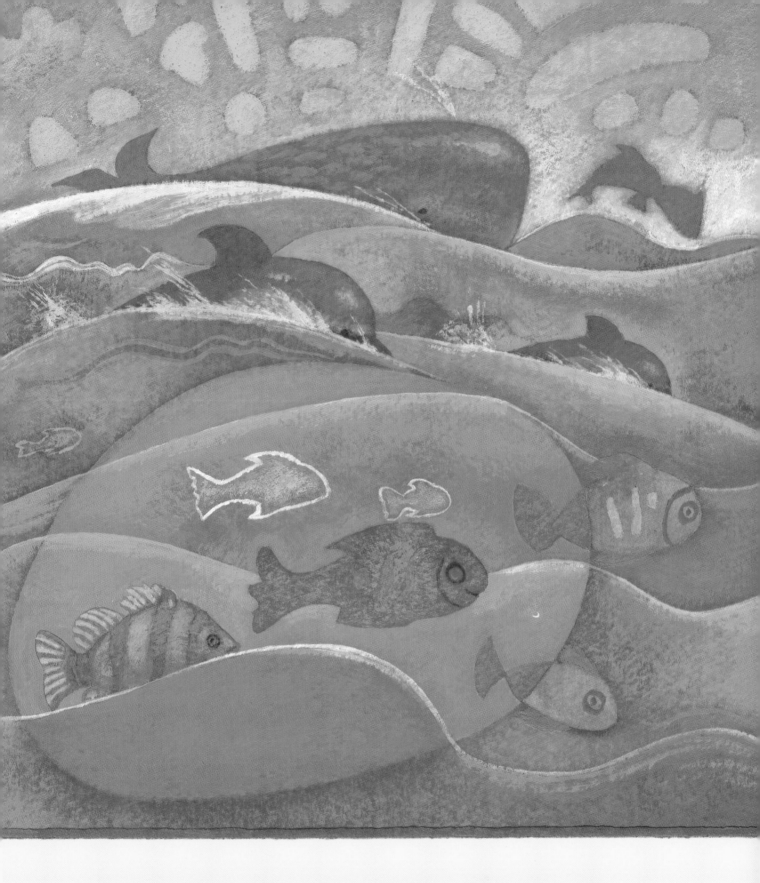

For it was the sea that had been hidden inside the pumpkin.
Out came the creatures: whales, dolphins, crabs, and sunfish. All
the people ran to the top of the mountain to hide in the forest
of green leaves.

"Will the whole earth be covered?" they cried.
Higher and higher the waters kept rising, up the sides of
the mountain.

But when the water reached the edge of the magic forest the
little boy had planted, it stopped.

The people peeked out from behind the leaves. And what did they see? Small streams running through the trees. A beach of golden sand. And the wide open ocean, sparkling all around them.

Now the people could drink from the cool streams and splash in the rippling waves. Now they could gather fish from the flowing tides and plant their crops.

The child laughed and sang as the sun shone down and breezes blew through the green leaves and rustled the many-colored flowers. Water had come to the earth!

And that is how, the Taino say, between the sun and the sparkling blue sea, their island home—Boriquén—came to be.

Nina Jaffe's acclaimed retellings of world folklore include *Patakin: World Tales of Drums and Drummers* (Cricket Books, 2001) and *Tales for the Seventh Day: A Collection of Sabbath Stories* (Scholastic, 2000). Her books have been honored with the Sydney Taylor Award, The Anne Izard Storyteller's Choice Award, and a Smithsonian Notable Book. Recent titles include four picture books for the DC Comics Wonder Woman series (HarperCollins, 2004). Ms. Jaffe is on the graduate faculty of Bank Street College of Education. She lives in the Bronx with her husband, Bob, and son Louis.

Enrique O. Sánchez is a talented fine artist and an accomplished illustrator with several books to his credit, including *Big Enough/Bastante grande* by Ofelia Dumas Lachtman (Piñata Books, 1998). He also owns an extensive drum collection. A conga player as well as an artist, he shares his passion for art and music with his son, Aron, who is also a musician and an artist. Sánchez lives in Vermont, with his wife, Joan, a modern dancer.

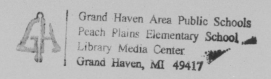